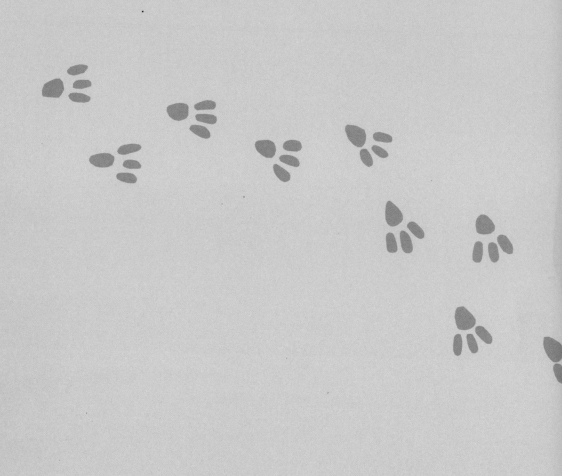

Jan Thomas

What Will FAT CAT Sit On?

Houghton Mifflin Harcourt

Boston   New York

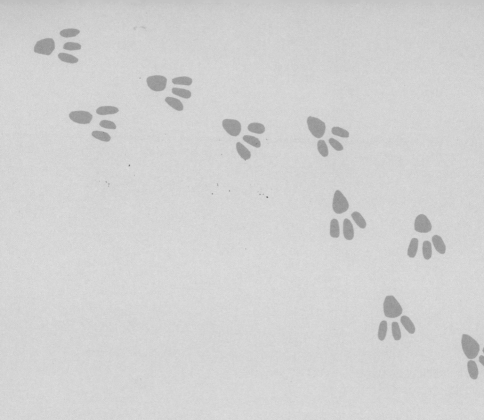

www.hmhco.com

The illustrations in this book were done digitally.

ISBN: 978-0-544-85004-0

Manufactured in China
SCP 10 9 8 7 6 5 4 3 2 1
4500700832

For Sam

What will Fat Cat sit on?

Will Fat Cat sit on...

NO!

Fat Cat will not sit on the

COW!

Will Fat Cat sit on...

NO!

Fat Cat will not sit on the

CHICKEN

(or the pig).

Yippee!

Will Fat Cat sit on...

the DOG?

Grrrr...

NO!

Fat Cat will not sit on the

DOG!

OKAY, so Fat Cat will

NOT

sit on the cow,
or the chicken,
or the pig,
or the dog.

Then ... what WILL

Fat Cat sit on?

Eeep?

Perhaps he could
sit on the
CHAIR?

The CHAIR! Of COURSE!

NOW,
what will Fat Cat . . .

have for LUNCH?

Get your child ready to read in three simple steps!

 **1** **I READ**	Read the book to your child.
2 **WE READ**	Read the book together.
 **3** **YOU READ**	Encourage your child to read the book over and over again.

Looking for more laughs?

Don't miss these other adventures
from Jan Thomas:

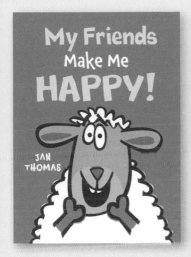

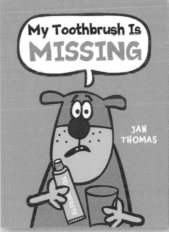

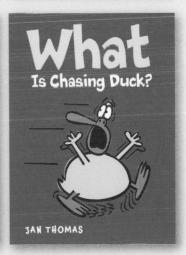